"Ding, ding! Ding, ding!"
Dad came into Chip's room. He was
ringing a bell. Chip sat up in bed.

"It's time to get up," said Dad. "Mum's
away and we have a lot of jobs to do."

1

Dad rang the bell on the stairs.

"Time to get up!" he called.

"Do we have to?" asked Biff. "It's the weekend."

"Yes," said Dad. "Mum gets back
tonight. The house is a mess. We must
tidy up."

"I suppose so," yawned Chip.

"Good. I'll start breakfast," said Dad.

The children came down for breakfast.
"Bad news," said Dad. "The milk has gone off, I've burned the toast and we've run out of juice. I'm sorry."

"Oh no!" said Kipper. "I'm hungry!"

"We'll have to go to the supermarket,"
said Dad. "We need some more food."
"I've got a better idea," said Chip.
"Let's have breakfast in the café."

"You can eat what you like," said Dad.
"Then we'll do the shopping."

"Hooray!" said Kipper. "I'm going
to have a big breakfast!"

"I'd like blueberry pancakes," said Biff.

"I want eggs," said Kipper.

"Why not have a kipper, Kipper?" said Chip.

"Only if you have chips, Chip!" said Kipper.

At home, Dad told the children to start their jobs.

"I'll put the shopping away," he said. "You go and tidy your rooms. That big breakfast should give you lots of energy."

The children looked at the mess.

"Let's tidy up later," said Chip.
"I'm so full, I can't move!"

"No chance of a walk then," thought
Floppy.

Just then, the magic key began to glow.

The magic took them back in time. It
took them to a big house. It took them into
a large hall with a big staircase.

"It's still dark outside," said Biff.

"Ding, ding!" A bell began to ring.

Suddenly, a door opened. A little
girl came in. She was holding a candle.
   "I'm Rose. You must be the new
servants. The housekeeper will see
you now. Follow me," she said.

Rose took them down a corridor into
a large storeroom. The housekeeper
was waiting for them.

"You are late," she said, sternly.
"There are lots of jobs to be done."

She gave the children lists of jobs.
"Begin with the cleaning," she said.
"It has to be done before breakfast.
Ah! I see you have brought a
dog. Good."

Rose took them to a large kitchen.

"This is Mrs Fry," said Rose. "She's
the cook."

"Hello," said Mrs Fry. "I see
you have brought a dog. Good."

"Why is everyone pleased that we have brought a dog?" asked Chip.
Mrs Fry pointed at a wooden wheel.
"Put your dog in here," she said.
"I may not like this," thought Floppy.

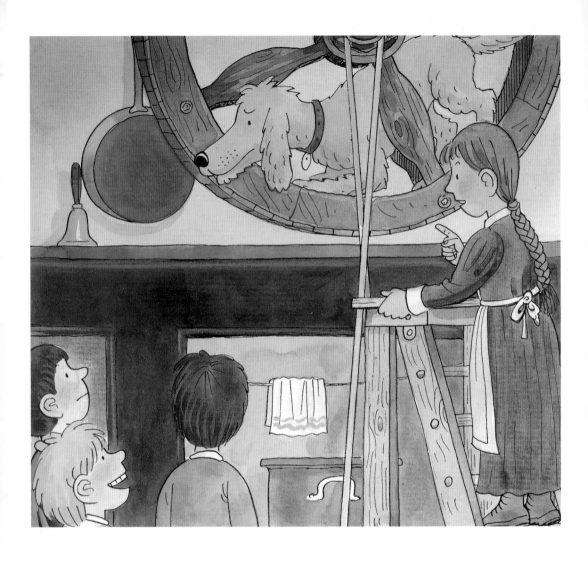

Rose put Floppy inside the wheel.

"The wheel turns the meat over the fire," said Rose. "It stops the meat burning."

"You look like a giant hamster," laughed Kipper.

"Now we must hurry, there's so much to do," said Rose. "Lord Plum will be up soon. We must finish the jobs, then we can get his breakfast ready."

Mrs Fry put the meat on the spit.
"We need this for Lord Plum's breakfast."
She looked at Floppy.
"Keep walking and don't stop!" she said.
"Funny way to get a walk," thought
Floppy.

"What else is for breakfast?" asked Biff.

"Kippers, oyster bread, beetroot pancakes, ale and ice-cream. Nothing too fancy," said Rose. "I'll get it ready. You get on with the jobs on the list."

Biff had to scrub the clothes clean.

She beat the rugs.

Then, she had to make some bread. . .

. . .and put powder on some wigs.

Chip had to clean all the fireplaces.

Then, he had to collect a lot of coal.

Next, he had to polish the silver. . .

. . .and polish all the boots.

Kipper churned milk to make butter.

He got ice cream from the icehouse.

He had to carry water to the bathrooms. . .

. . .and scrub all the floors.

"Come quickly," said Rose. "The food is ready. We must take it to the dining room."

"Hurry up and don't forget Lord Plum's newspaper," said Mrs Fry.

The children put out the dishes on a
big table.

"Hurry up," said the housekeeper.
"Lord Plum will be down soon. He
won't want to see you in here."

At last, breakfast was finished.

"Was Lord Plum happy with his breakfast?" asked Kipper.

"No!" said the housekeeper. "You forgot to iron his newspaper!"

"I'm worn out," said Kipper.

"I never want another walk," said Floppy.

"At least we can have a rest now," said Chip.

"A rest?" said Rose. "We have to
start getting ready for lunch!"

Suddenly, the magic key began to glow.
It was time to go home.

"What a relief!" said Biff.

"That was hard work," said Biff.
Dad came into Biff's room.

"Hurry up," he said. "We've still got lots
of jobs to do. Then we have to walk
Floppy."

"Oh no!" said everyone.

Early next morning, the children
made Mum a surprise breakfast.

"What a big breakfast!" said Mum.
"You have gone to so much trouble."

"It was nothing," said Biff.